W9-CEA-584

Outback Odyssey

Adventures of Riley®

Outback Odyssey

Dear Riley,

Australia's koalas are losing their trees! The eucalyptus trees they need for food and shelter are being chopped down to make room for cities and farms.

We have to find ways to save the koala's habitat, or koalas may become extinct!

Your Aunt Martha, Cousin Alice, and I will be doing our research at an Australian sheep station, where we'll learn how to be real Australian cowboys!

Ready, pardner?

Uncle Max

BY

Amanda Lumry

AND

Laura Hurwitz

SCHOLASTIC PRESS ★ NEW YORK

A special thank-you to all the scientists who collaborated on this project. Your time and assistance are very much appreciated.

Copyright © by Eaglemont Press 2009

All rights reserved. Published by Scholastic Inc., *Publishers since 1920.* SCHOLASTIC, SCHOLASTIC PRESS, and associated logos are trademarks and/or registered trademarks of Scholastic Inc.

No part of this publication may be reproduced, stored in a retrieval system, or transmitted in any form or by any means, electronic, mechanical, photocopying, recording, or otherwise, without written permission of the publisher. For information regarding permission, write to Eaglemont Press, PMB 741, 15600 NE 8th #B-1, Bellevue, WA 98008.

www.eaglemont.com

All photographs by Amanda Lumry except:
Page 3 red kangaroo © Art Wolfe/Getty Images
Page 6 mulgara, page 24 river red gum trees, page 27 dingo © Jason Edwards/Getty Images
Page 12 kookaburra © Cyril Laubscher/Getty Images
Page 25 dingo © Nicole Duplaix/Getty Images

Illustrations and Layouts by Ulkutay & Ulkutay, London WC2E 9RZ
Editing and Digital Compositing by Michael E. Penman
Digital Imaging by Quebecor World Premedia

Library of Congress Control Number: 2003105372

ISBN-13: 978-0-545-06845-1
ISBN-10: 0-545-06845-2

10 9 8 7 6 5 4 3 2 1 09 10 11 12 13

Printed in Singapore 46
First Scholastic printing, May 2009

A portion of the proceeds from your purchase of this licensed product supports the stated educational mission of the Smithsonian Institution – "the increase and diffusion of knowledge." The name of the Smithsonian Institution and the sunburst logo are registered trademarks of the Smithsonian Institution and are registered in the U.S. Patent and Trademark Office. www.si.edu

2% of the proceeds from this book will be donated to the Wildlife Conservation Society. http://wcs.org

We try to produce the most beautiful books possible and we are extremely concerned about the impact of our manufacturing process on the forests of the world and the environment as a whole. Accordingly, we made sure that the paper used in this book has been certified as coming from forests that are managed to ensure the protection of the people and wildlife dependent upon them.

"Mom, can I watch TV?" asked Riley.

"After you finish your homework," said his mother.

Riley looked at his assignment. He was only halfway done. *That's probably good enough*, he thought. Besides, his favorite show was on!

A week later, Riley met Cousin Alice and Uncle Max at the London airport for the long flight to Australia.

"We'll meet up with Aunt Martha in Alice Springs. She is already there studying the local cultures and languages," said Uncle Max.

Red Kangaroo

- It can't walk. It can only hop.
- It is the world's largest marsupial.
- It lives in small groups called mobs.
- It can find water using smell alone.
- Although called a red kangaroo, the male is usually reddish-brown and the female is usually bluish-gray.

—Robert D. Fisher, Collections Manager, Mammals, National Museum of Natural History, Smithsonian Institution

"There's the **outback**," said Uncle Max, as their plane approached Alice Springs.

"I don't see any houses," said Alice.

"Not many people can live out here," said Uncle Max. "There's hardly any water, and it gets very hot."

Aunt Martha met them at the airport and they all climbed into her jeep. "We'll fly to the sheep station, which is a kind of ranch, tomorrow," she said. "I have a big surprise for everyone first."

After driving for about four hours, an enormous rock mountain came into view.

"That's Uluru," said Aunt Martha. "It's also called Ayers Rock."

"Wow! Let's climb it!" cried Riley.

"Uluru has special meaning to the local Aboriginal culture, and they prefer that tourists don't climb it," said Aunt Martha.

"We can walk up close to it, though," said Uncle Max.

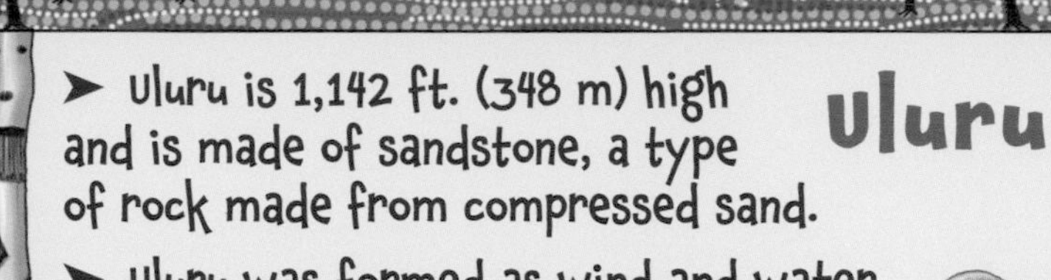

Uluru

➤ Uluru is 1,142 ft. (348 m) high and is made of sandstone, a type of rock made from compressed sand.

➤ Uluru was formed as wind and water eroded and lowered the land around it.

➤ Uluru's markings are a result of strong desert winds blowing sand across its surface. The sand cuts into the rock and creates interesting shapes. —William Melson, Research Scientist Emeritus, Smithsonian Institution

Mulgara

- It lives in underground burrows during the day to escape the heat.
- It is a nighttime hunter of small **prey**, including insects, spiders, mice, and lizards.
- It may live in a short, single burrow, or a burrow with lots of tunnels and up to six entrances.

—Kristofer M. Helgen, Ph.D., Research Zoologist and Curator of Mammals, Division of Mammals, Smithsonian Institution

Something furry brushed by Alice's leg. "Ack!" she yelled.

"It's okay," said Uncle Max. "That's a mulgara, a desert-dwelling marsupial, or mammal with an external pouch, like a kangaroo or koala," he said.

"Speaking of koalas, where are they?" asked Riley.

"Koalas can't live here in central Australia," said Uncle Max. "They only eat the leaves of eucalyptus trees, which grow in the eastern and southern parts of Australia."

The setting sun turned Uluru bright red. The family drove to a local hotel to spend the night.

In the morning, they drove back to the airport. A **willy-willy** swirled in the distance.

"I'll be flying us to the sheep station in this **eco-friendly** plane," said Aunt Martha. "It runs on fuel made from sugarcane, which doesn't pollute the atmosphere as much as gasoline."

"Gasoline **emissions** cause increased temperatures and **drought**. Koalas won't eat from eucalyptus trees damaged by **drought**, so what's good for the atmosphere is also good for koalas," said Uncle Max.

Wedge-Tailed Eagle

➤ It is Australia's largest bird of **prey**.

➤ Its wingspan is over 8.2 ft. (2.5 m).

➤ It has great eyesight and can even see **infrared** and **ultraviolet light**.

➤ To hunt, it may team up with other birds to cause goats to fall off steep hills, or drive flocks of sheep or kangaroos to find the weakest ones to attack.

—Barney Long,
Senior Program Officer,
Asian Species Conservation,
World Wildlife Fund

Looking down, they saw the **landscape** change from sandy desert to green forests and grass.

"Look at all those kangaroos!" cried Riley. "Why is the area next to them so black?"

"Brush fires," said Uncle Max. "Large parts of the Australian **outback** are barren, so brush fires are almost impossible to control or contain. When eucalyptus forests catch fire, the koalas lose their food and their homes. Sometimes entire koala populations completely disappear."

Gray Kangaroo

- An adult male is called a boomer or an old man. An adult female is called a doe or a flyer. A baby kangaroo is called a joey.
- A male can jump 33 ft. (10 m) in one leap.
- A female can have three babies at one time, but it gets pretty crowded in her pouch!

—Sybille Klenzendorf, Ph.D., Director—Species Conservation, World Wildlife Fund

Aunt Martha landed the plane on a dirt airstrip. A man was waiting for them.

"Riley, here's another surprise for you. This is my cousin, Oscar Plimpton! He runs the sheep station with his wife, Robin," said Uncle Max.

"Robin can't wait to see you all," said Oscar. "Pile in and we'll be on our way. This is my daughter, Hayley."

"What a cute lamb!" Alice said.

"It's a poddy lamb," said Hayley. "That means it's an orphan. I have to be her mother until she's old enough to feed herself."

Over dinner, Oscar told them about life at Plimpton Station.

"I didn't know what to expect when I bought this sheep station," Oscar said. "It's bad enough that Australia has the least **fertile** soil on Earth, but now many sheep and cattle stations are barely surviving because of increased **drought**, brush fires, soil **erosion**, and overgrazing."

"The **outback** is definitely facing more challenges than ever before," said Uncle Max. "And so are koalas."

"The good news is that I've been working on some ideas that should help other **outback** residents like ourselves—and koalas," said Oscar.

That night, Riley dreamed of an Australia where cities, farms, and koalas all lived happily together under the cool shadow of Uluru and eucalyptus forests.

Suddenly, a tiny kangaroo jumped out of Riley's dream and onto his bed. Before he could fully wake up, Alice and Hayley burst into his room.

"Riley! Jackaroos and jillaroos rise with the sun," said Alice.

"Jacka-whos?" Riley asked, more confused than ever.

"Jackaroos are Aussie boy ranch hands, and jillaroos are girls," said Hayley.

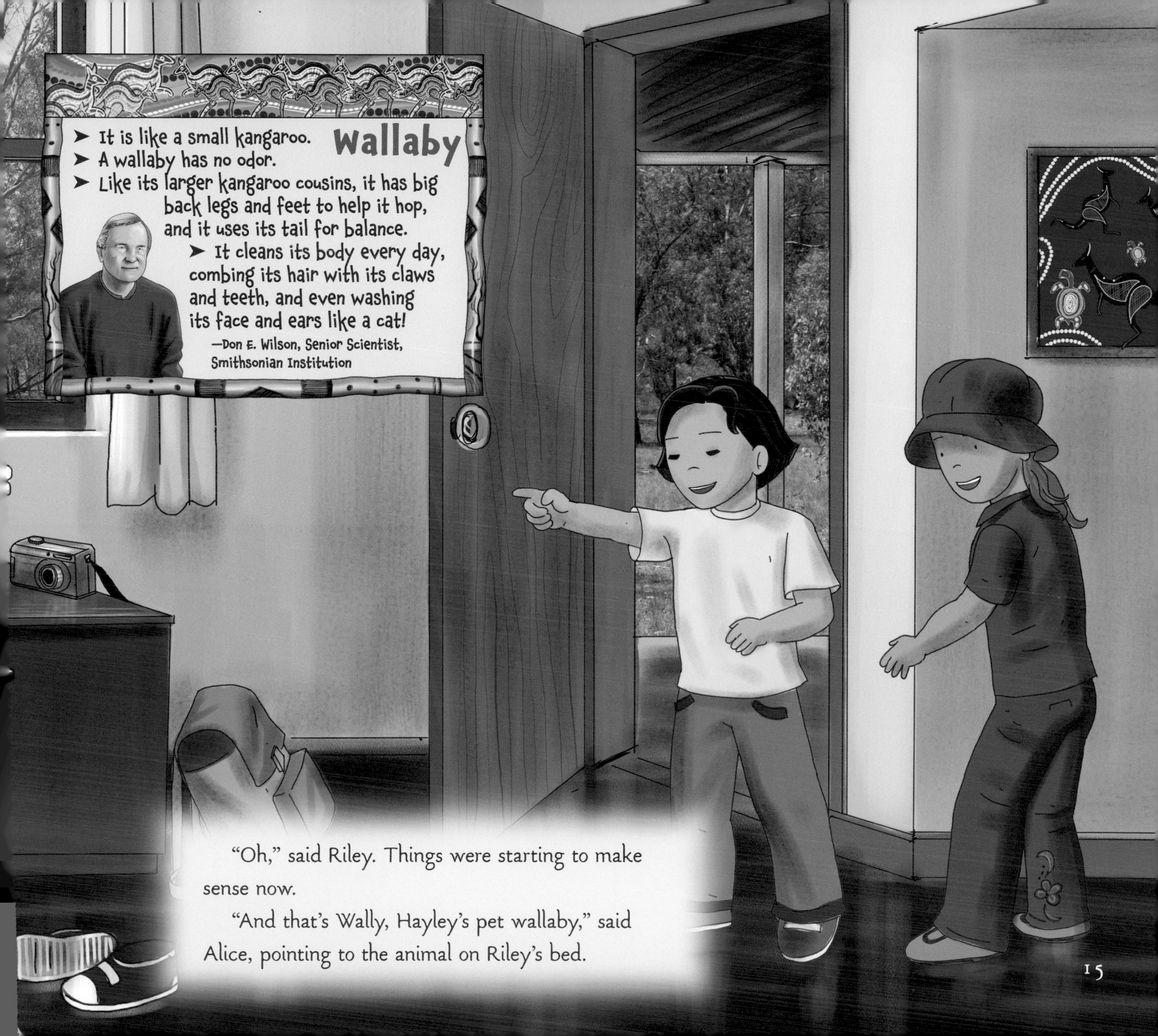

"Oh," said Riley. Things were starting to make sense now.

"And that's Wally, Hayley's pet wallaby," said Alice, pointing to the animal on Riley's bed.

Riley walked outside and got his first good look at the incredibly large sheep **pasture**.

"Here," said Oscar. "This is how we dress for work."

After walking through the **pasture** gate, Oscar asked Riley to close and latch the gate behind them.

"There have been dingo sightings all around here, and we can't afford to lose even one sheep to them."

Alice yelled, "Come on, slowpoke!"

Riley quickly closed the gate, but didn't take the time to latch it. *That's probably good enough*, he thought. *I need to catch up with the others. . . .*

Oscar and Robin spent the morning showing Riley and Alice around the sheep station. They got to crack the warning whip used for getting the sheep's attention . . .

. . . shear a sheep . . .

. . . practice riding horses . . .

. . . learn how to throw a boomerang . . .

. . . direct the sheep dogs to corral the sheep . . .

. . . and lasso fence posts using a **lariat**!

"Twirl it, toss it, and pull it back to tie it!" said Oscar. "It's trickier than it looks." Riley had almost gotten the hang of it when Uncle Max showed up to talk with Oscar.

Everyone got on their horses and rode toward the nearby hills.

"See all these eucalyptus trees, Max?" asked Oscar. "I figured that since 80 percent of Australia's eucalyptus forests have been cleared for cities and farms, it was my job as a farmer to plant more before they're all gone. And would you look at that—there's a young koala on that tree right next to us!"

"The fact that this one is young tells me there are probably other koalas nearby. Koalas are **solitary** animals, but joeys will often stay in the home range of their mothers for up to three years," said Uncle Max.

"I like that you use windmills," said Aunt Martha. "Wind energy is a plentiful resource, and it doesn't harm the environment."

Part of Uncle Max's mission was to check the size and health of the local koala population. The group counted every koala in sight. They found eight koalas in Oscar's eucalyptus trees. Most of them were sleeping.

"I'm not surprised," said Uncle Max. "They sleep 16 hours a day or more."

In the distance, they heard a dog barking.

"That sounds like Otto, our lead sheepdog," said Hayley.

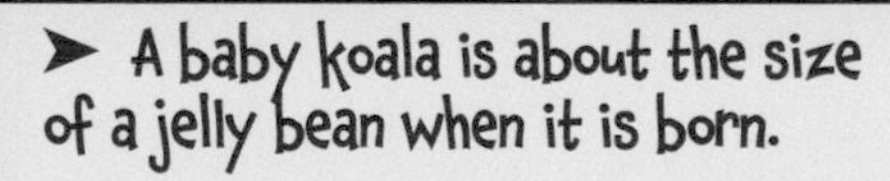

Koala

- A baby koala is about the size of a jelly bean when it is born.
- It makes a noise called a bellow that sounds like a pig snorting or a person burping!
- The male koala has a scent **gland** on its chest that becomes very smelly in the springtime to attract female koalas.
- A koala may look cute and cuddly, but it will readily scratch and bite.

—Jennifer Tobey, Research Coordinator, CRES, San Diego Zoological Society

Oscar led them to a rushing creek.

"What has a duck's bill, webbed feet, and a flat tail like a beaver?" asked Riley.

"A platypus, of course!" answered Uncle Max. "Great spotting, Carrot Top."

"What I've done here is plant river red gum trees along the banks," said Oscar. "Their roots hold the soil in place so it won't **erode** and pollute the water. They also provide food and shelter for animals like the platypus you just saw."

Just then, Robin galloped up.

"The sheep are making a lot of noise," she said. "We'd better check on them."

Platypus

- It is one of the only mammals that lays eggs.
- Its favorite foods are worms and insects.
- The male platypus has a poisonous spike on each heel. A platypus is usually shy, though, and would rather hide than attack.
- Its burrows are built next to water and can be up to 98 ft. (30 m) long.

—Helen Kafka, Museum Technician, Division of Mammals, National Museum of Natural History, Smithsonian Institution

From a distance they saw that the **pasture** gate was open. Two wild dogs **lurked** nearby.

"Oh no, DINGOES!" shouted Oscar.

"Oh no! The poddy lamb!" shouted Robin.

"We'll never get there in time!" said Hayley, starting to cry.

This is my fault, thought Riley, digging his heels in and galloping as fast as he could. *I shouldn't have been in such a hurry to close the gate.* He grasped his **lariat** firmly in his hand. *Maybe this time I can throw it straight.*

The dingoes saw Riley charging toward them and ran for the poddy lamb. There was no way Riley would get there in time. Suddenly, a bright pink object shot by Riley's head. It flew over the dingoes, curved around, and disappeared behind him. The dingoes stopped in their tracks. It was Alice's boomerang! Now was his chance! Twirling the **lariat** around his head once, twice, three times, he threw it with all his might. . . .

Dingo

- It mainly eats rabbits and wallabies, but will also feed on lizards, insects, birds, marsupial mice, and, of course, sheep.
- It is not a native Aussie! It was brought to Australia by Southeast Asian **seafarers** between 3,500 and 5,000 years ago.
- A mother dingo drinks water, then **regurgitates** it for her pup back in their den.

—Dave Schmidt, Museum Specialist, Division of Mammals, Smithsonian Institution

The circle of rope looped perfectly over the top of the gate.

SLAM!

Riley pulled the gate shut before the dingoes could get in. Cut off from their **prey**, and with everyone else's horses galloping closer, the dingoes ran off.

"Riley! Alice! That was amazing!" said Hayley.

"Great job, both of you!" said Oscar. "Riley, you're a natural jackaroo!"

"I think a real jackaroo would have locked the gate to begin with," said Uncle Max.

Riley turned beet red. "I'm sorry. I thought pushing it closed was good enough."

"Directions are made to be followed," said Uncle Max. "But I think you've learned your lesson."

"And lucky for the poddy lamb, your new skills saved the day," said Oscar, looking at Riley and Alice. "What do you say, mates, shall we count some more koalas?"

That night, they sat around the barbeque, or *barbie*, as Robin called it. They enjoyed billie tea and damper bread as Oscar did his best to play a didgeridoo. Riley, Alice, and Hayley took turns feeding the poddy lamb.

"Today we counted twelve koalas," said Uncle Max. "Oscar's idea of planting more eucalyptus trees is working beautifully!"

"Planting native trees not only reduces soil **erosion**, but it creates natural **barriers** against brush fires, too," added Oscar.

"Wow! Just look at the night sky," said Aunt Martha.

"There's a shooting star!" said Alice. "Make a wish."

Riley knew his trip was coming to an end, so he wished he could return to Plimpton Station soon.

When they finished their mission, it was clear that more eucalyptus trees, and more space to plant them, meant healthier koala populations and healthier farmland. Back at home, Riley told everyone about Uluru, Plimpton Station, and the dingoes. He also finished his homework.

Riley returned to living the life of a nine-year-old, until he once again heard from Uncle Max.

Where will Riley go next?

Further Information

Glossary

barriers: walls or other obstacles that keep things from getting from one place to another

drought: when there is no rain for a long time

eco-friendly: something that is kind to the environment

emissions: gases released from a source

erosion: the process of being worn away over time, usually by wind and/or water

fertile: when soil is healthy and able to produce many crops or plants

gland: an organ that makes and releases a substance inside an animal's body

infrared and **ultraviolet light:** special colors in the rainbow that people can't see

landscape: the visible features of an area of land

lariat: a rope used by ranchers that is looped and thrown to capture livestock

lurked: stayed hidden, waiting to jump out

outback: the dry, flat inland region of Australia

pasture: an area where animals eat grasses

prey: an animal hunted by another for food

regurgitates: brings partly digested food from the stomach back into the mouth

seafarers: people who regularly cross oceans to reach distant lands.

solitary: alone, apart from others

willy-willy: an Australian term for a dust devil, which is like a very small tornado

Alternative Energy

The oil we use to fuel most transportation and to heat our homes is fossil fuel that will someday run out. Alternative energy sources—such as biofuel cells that produce electricity using ordinary air mixed with hydrogen, solar cells powered by the sun, new forms of wind energy, and even batteries fueled by sugar—are all being developed. Soon everything, from computers to ocean liners, could be powered by renewable alternatives to oil. It's all about finding new, cleaner, and sustainable ways to power our world!

Australia

Indonesia
New Guinea
INDIAN OCEAN
CORAL SEA
Northern Territory
Alice Springs
Ayers Rock
Queensland
Western Australia
South Australia
Sheep Station
New South Wales
Victoria
INDIAN OCEAN
TASMAN SEA
Tasmania
N
W
E
S

Boomerang

A curved, wooden stick originally used by Aboriginal people that, when thrown correctly, returns to the thrower.

Didgeridoo

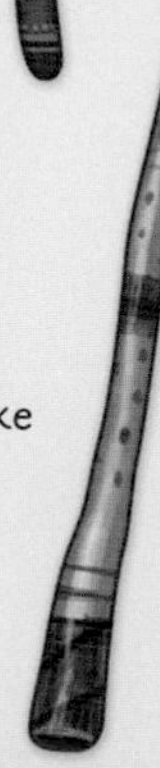

Aboriginal people have been playing this tubelike instrument—thought to be the oldest wind instrument—at ceremonies and dances for about 1,500 years.

JOIN US FOR MORE GREAT ADVENTURES!

RILEY'S WORLD™

Visit our Web site at

www.adventuresofriley.com

to find out how you can join Riley's super kids' club!

Look for these other great Riley books:

- Safari in South Africa
- Project Panda
- South Pole Penguins
- Polar Bear Puzzle
- Dolphins in Danger
- Tigers in Terai